Unstoppable Me

Susan Verde

Pictures by
Andrew Joyner

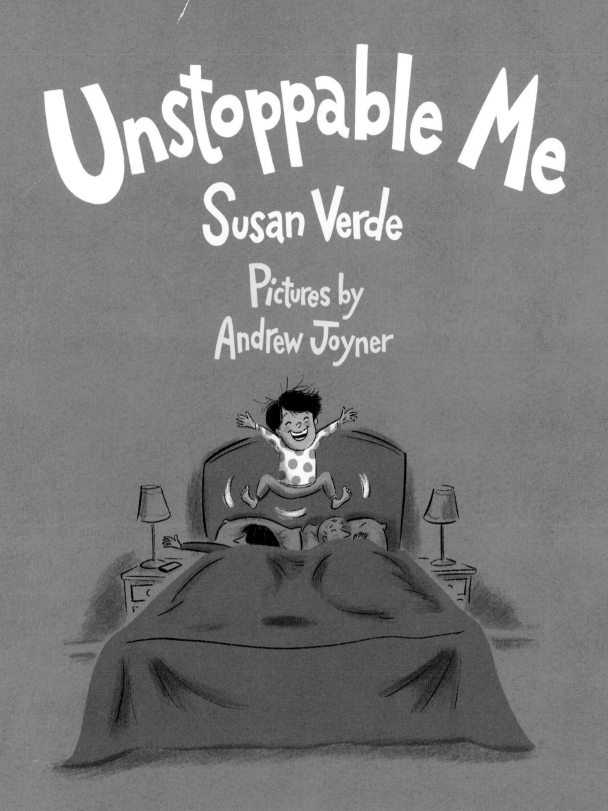

FARRAR STRAUS GIROUX

New York

I am movement

Heat

Static electricity

Fueled by food

Powered by **PLAY!**

Friendship

Compliments

Love and laughter

All these give me a
Turbo Boost!

I am environmentally friendly

No batteries required

No coal, no oil

Just a little water
to keep my engine
running

I can:
Bounce

Spin

Tumble

Dig

Create

Build

Knock down

Rebuild

No chair!

Slow down?

Sure, I can take a
moment to recharge

But when I'm ready
and powered up again…

WATCH ME GO!

I am perpetual motion

I'm a supersonic dreamer!

I can leap, soar, and
reach for the stars

Use what I've got

And you could light up

THE WORLD!

Author's Note

There are some kids who just can't sit still. Their bodies need movement in order for them to learn, explore, and find joy in their lives. I am a mom to one of these kids, and as a former elementary school teacher, I have had many of them in my classroom. Often, children who have trouble sitting and containing their energy for long periods of time are seen as disruptive or difficult. I was inspired to write this story as a way of approaching this amazing exuberance from a different perspective. I believe that if we can view a child's seemingly boundless energy as positive and something to celebrate, then we can help these kids love themselves just as they are. When children see their challenges as strengths and possibilities, they are less likely to "act out" and more likely to find success. With my own son, we have come up with many fun and useful ways to embrace his need to move and channel his energy. Sometimes it is exhausting, but it's always worth the effort.

All children have something incredible to offer, and each is amazingly unique. *Unstoppable Me* is meant to show all of the beautiful, special, and miraculous things about being a kid on the move!

To all the kids full of bright and shining energy, and to the amazing adults who help them light up the world! —S.V.

For Charlie —A.J.

Farrar Straus Giroux Books for Young Readers
An imprint of Macmillan Publishing Group, LLC
120 Broadway, New York, NY 10271

Text copyright © 2019 by Susan Verde
Pictures copyright © 2019 by Andrew Joyner
All rights reserved

Color separations by Bright Arts (H.K.) Ltd.
Printed in China by RR Donnelley Asia Printing Solutions Ltd.,
Dongguan City, Guangdong Province

Designed by Christina Dacanay
First edition, 2019

1 3 5 7 9 10 8 6 4 2

mackids.com

Library of Congress Control Number: 2018955248

Our books may be purchased in bulk for promotional, educational, or business use. Please contact your local bookseller or the Macmillan Corporate and Premium Sales Department at (800) 221-7945 ext. 5442 or by e-mail at MacmillanSpecialMarkets@macmillan.com.

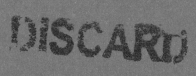